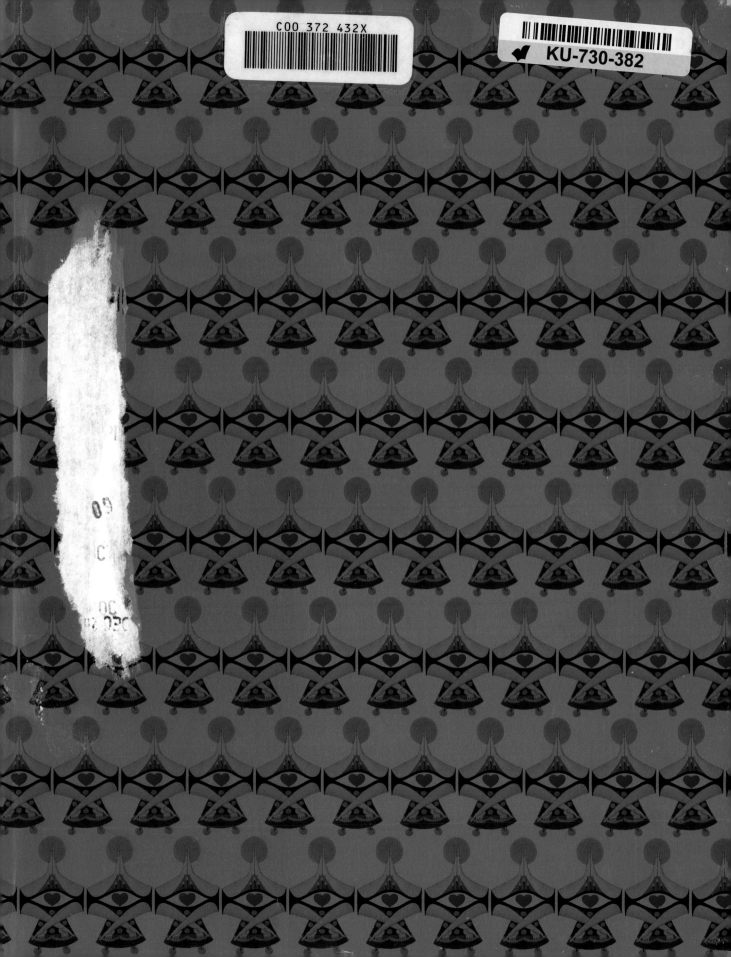

This book belongs to

Yakov and the Seven Thieves

by

Madonna

Art by

Gennady Spirin

PUFFIN

A CALLAWAY EDITION

This book is dedicated to
naughty children everywhere.

MADONNA

ONCE UPON A TIME, IN A VERY
small village tucked away between two mountains, there lived
a cobbler named Yakov. From the window of his workshop, he would
marvel at the natural beauty surrounding him – the magical forests,
the crystal-clear streams and the majestic snowcapped mountains
that rose before him in the distance.

Yakov had a young son named Mikhail who was so ill that he could
not leave his bed and so weak that he could neither move nor speak.
Yakov and his wife, Olga, had spent the last year speaking to doctors
and searching for a cure. But their son's illness remained a mystery.
Yakov realized that it was time to take matters into his own hands.

He knelt at the side of his son's bed and, wiping the sweat from his brow, he reassured him, saying, "Do not worry, my son. You will see. Everything will be fine."

Mikhail was too sick to respond. Olga looked up with tears in her eyes, and left the room quickly so her son would not see her cry. Yakov followed his wife out of the room and found her standing behind the door, weeping.

"We must not give up so easily," he said, wiping the tears from her face.

Olga could not bear to see her son suffer any longer. "He is leaving this world," she said with great sadness in her voice. "I can see it in his eyes."

Yakov knew there was truth in what she said, but he was not prepared to give up yet. "He is a strong boy," he offered.

"Strength will not help him. Only a miracle can save him now," responded his wife.

She was right.

"You must go and seek advice from the wise old man who lives in the last house at the edge of the village," pleaded Olga. "People say that he speaks to angels and that he can perform miracles."

"ut we do not know him," answered Yakov.

"Knock on his door and offer him money," replied Olga. "He will have mercy when he learns that Mikhail is our only child."

So Yakov gathered all the money they had in the world and set off to see the wise old man who lived in the last house at the edge of the village.

When Yakov arrived, he knocked on the door, which was opened by a small boy, not much older than Mikhail.

"Hello," said the boy with big green eyes. "I am Pavel."

"Hello, Pavel. Is your father in?" asked Yakov.

"No, but my grandfather is," answered Pavel. "Whom shall I say is calling?"

"I am Yakov the cobbler," he replied. "He does not know me, but it is urgent that I speak to him."

A kind voice could be heard over Pavel's shoulder.

"Come in, Yakov, and share some of my fresh dates," said the old man.

Yakov was relieved to see that the old man's face was as gentle as his voice, and he took off his hat and went inside.

The old man could hear the worry in Yakov's voice and tried to put him at ease: "Please sit down and tell me what disturbs you."

akov sat down in a comfortable chair and told the wise old man all about his only son – how sick he was, how they had searched without any success for a cure, and how he could sense the Angel of Death hovering above his son's bed. After Yakov finished, the old man closed his eyes and said nothing.

Yakov did not move or breathe. He just waited with hope in his heart.

After a few moments, the old man said, "I will see what I can do."

"I am not rich," said Yakov. "Even so, everything I have is yours, and I am happy to give it to you."

Yakov opened his leather bag of coins and notes, but the old man put his hand out to stop Yakov's offer.

"That will not be necessary," said the old man. "But if I am successful, my grandson Pavel could do with a new pair of shoes."

"Thank you. Thank you so very much!" Yakov exclaimed.

The old man could see that Yakov was still overcome with worry and sadness, and he tried again to reassure him. "I will pray tonight and see what the angels have to say. Now, go home and try to get some rest. We will speak in the morning."

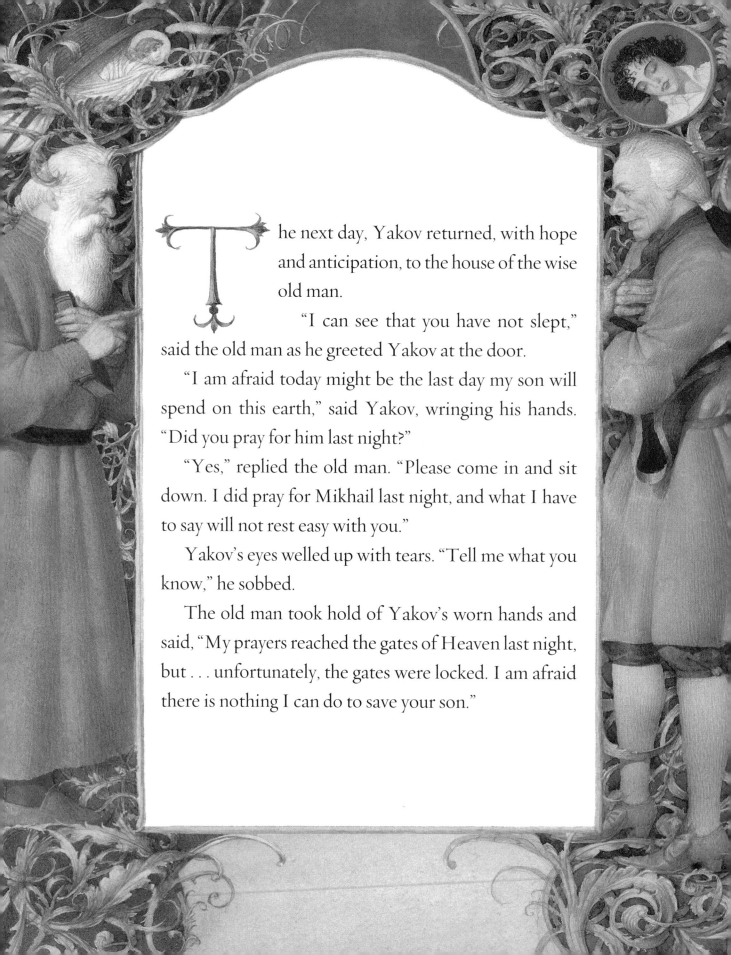

The next day, Yakov returned, with hope and anticipation, to the house of the wise old man.

"I can see that you have not slept," said the old man as he greeted Yakov at the door.

"I am afraid today might be the last day my son will spend on this earth," said Yakov, wringing his hands. "Did you pray for him last night?"

"Yes," replied the old man. "Please come in and sit down. I did pray for Mikhail last night, and what I have to say will not rest easy with you."

Yakov's eyes welled up with tears. "Tell me what you know," he sobbed.

The old man took hold of Yakov's worn hands and said, "My prayers reached the gates of Heaven last night, but . . . unfortunately, the gates were locked. I am afraid there is nothing I can do to save your son."

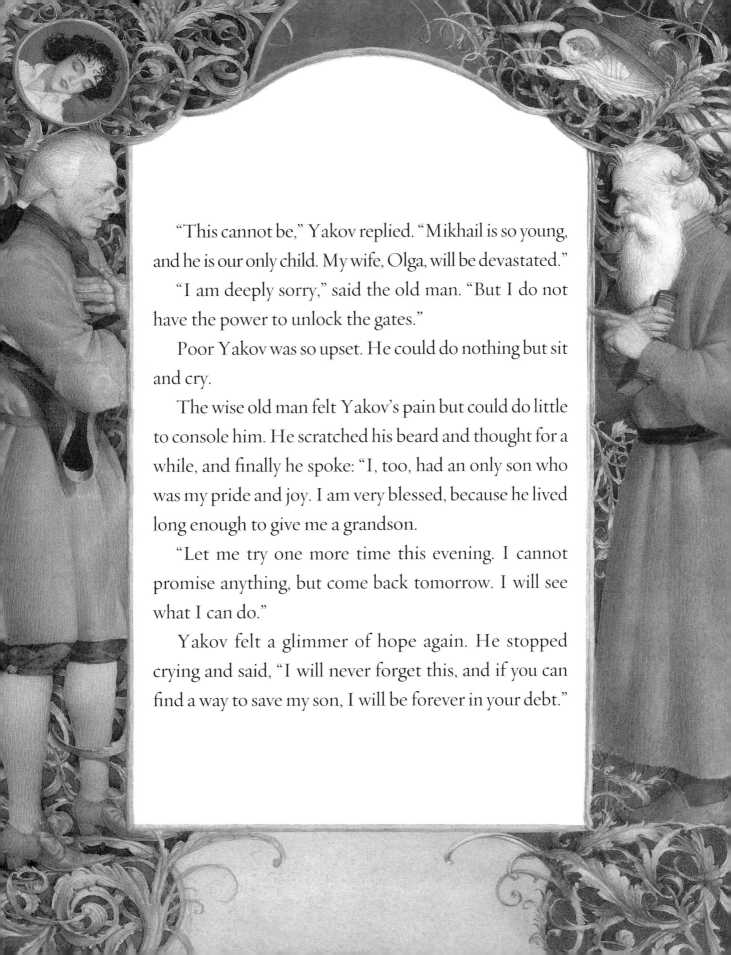

"This cannot be," Yakov replied. "Mikhail is so young, and he is our only child. My wife, Olga, will be devastated."

"I am deeply sorry," said the old man. "But I do not have the power to unlock the gates."

Poor Yakov was so upset. He could do nothing but sit and cry.

The wise old man felt Yakov's pain but could do little to console him. He scratched his beard and thought for a while, and finally he spoke: "I, too, had an only son who was my pride and joy. I am very blessed, because he lived long enough to give me a grandson.

"Let me try one more time this evening. I cannot promise anything, but come back tomorrow. I will see what I can do."

Yakov felt a glimmer of hope again. He stopped crying and said, "I will never forget this, and if you can find a way to save my son, I will be forever in your debt."

hen Yakov left the house, the old man called his grandson to his side and made a very strange request. "I want you to go into town and find all the thieves, pickpockets and criminals who live there. Then I want you to bring them to me. The worse they are, the better."

Pavel's big green eyes grew even bigger. "But, Grandfather," he said, "isn't that dangerous?"

The wise old man put his hand on his heart and said, "You must trust me."

So Pavel went into town and gathered all the thieves and pickpockets he could find. He was surprised by how easy it was to locate them and how willing they were to come with him. Even they had heard of the wise old man who lived in the very last house at the edge of the village. They, too, had heard he could talk to angels and, for that very reason, they had never bothered him.

When the thieves arrived at his house, the old man invited them in and offered them drinks and places to sit. He went round the room and asked them their names and what they specialized in.

ladimir the Villain spoke first. He was big and fat and hairy. He claimed that he could bend metal with his bare hands and punch holes through walls made of stone.

And then spoke Sadko the Snake. He was thin as a stick and sharp as a rake. There wasn't a lock that he couldn't pick or a jewel that he wouldn't take.

There was Boris the Barefoot Midget. He liked to run through the streets snatching old ladies' handbags and small children's toys, which he kept for himself. (But he was afraid of the dark, you see, so he only stole during the day.)

And Stinky Pasha, who specialized in taking other people's horses and sheep without paying for them. Eventually, he started to smell like them. (Horses and sheep, that is.)

Next in line was Petra the Pickpocket. She dressed like a boy, but she was, in fact, a very naughty girl. She loved to tell long, made-up stories about terrible things that never really happened. While the listeners were held spellbound by her fibs, Petra would sneak into their pockets with her long, spidery fingers and take whatever she could find. Her fingers were everywhere they were not supposed to be – especially in her nose.

Then there was Ivan the Arsonist, who had a wooden leg and liked to set fire to barns and cornfields and sometimes, accidentally, his own leg.

And last, but not least, there was Igor the Tiger, who didn't live up to his name, and whose worst crime in life was that he sat around all day doing absolutely nothing.

There were seven slippery scoundrels in all. They entertained each other for a while with their boasting and their bragging until, finally, the old man spoke.

"I have invited you to my home for a very special reason. I would like you all to pray with me."

The thieves looked at one another and laughed uproariously, except for Boris the Barefoot Midget, who was staring longingly at Pavel's sandals, until Ivan the Arsonist kicked him in the shin with his wooden leg.

"Owwwww!" shouted Boris. "You hurt me. That was not very nice."

"Show some respect, short stuff, or I will set your toes on fire," growled Ivan.

When they had all finished belching and farting and behaving like twits, they grew very quiet. They could see that the old man was serious, and something about him commanded their respect.

"I have asked you all here for a very precise purpose," he said. "Yakov the cobbler's only son is very, very sick. He might not make it through the night, and he needs your help. I would like you all to pray for him." The old man looked around the room into each of their eyes. They were spellbound by this mysterious old man who could talk to angels. Was he a wizard? Could he make miracles happen? Did he have magical powers?

No one knew for sure.

In any case, it did not matter, because (even though they were all a couple of sandwiches short of a picnic) they could tell that the old man was sincere.

And then something very peculiar happened: they all closed their eyes and bowed their heads in prayer.

The next day, as soon as the sun came up, there was a lot of banging on the old man's door.

"I'm coming, I'm coming," yawned Pavel, stumbling out of bed and rubbing his eyes.

The old man was right behind him. They opened the door, and there stood Yakov. He did not need to say a single word, because his joyful face told the whole story.

"I can tell that you have brought me good news," said the old man. "How wonderful it is to see you smile!"

"Thank you! Thank you! How can I ever repay you?" exclaimed Yakov. "My son has never looked better. It is as though he had not been sick at all. My wife and I are overjoyed and forever grateful! It is a miracle! A miracle has taken place!"

"Yes, indeed it has," said the old man. "Now go home and rest. I know you have not slept in days."

Yakov knelt down and gently kissed the old man's hand. Then he presented Pavel with a beautiful pair of green shoes that matched the boy's eyes. And before Pavel could say thank you, Yakov danced away down the road.

The old man was about to go back to bed, when Pavel stopped him and asked, "How can this be, Grandfather? You are so good and honest and pure, and the people who I brought back yesterday were cheats and liars and thieves – the opposite of you! Could you not have asked better people back to our home to pray with you and help you unlock the gates of Heaven?"

It was a good question.

The old man looked at Pavel with a twinkle in his eye, and said, "Sit down, and I will explain it to you. When I prayed on the first night for Yakov's son, I reached the gates of Heaven, but they were locked shut, and there was nothing I could do. Yakov's heart was broken, and I felt his pain. How could I give up?

"Suddenly, a thought came to me, and I asked you to round up all the rascals and thieves in the village and bring them to our home to pray with me."

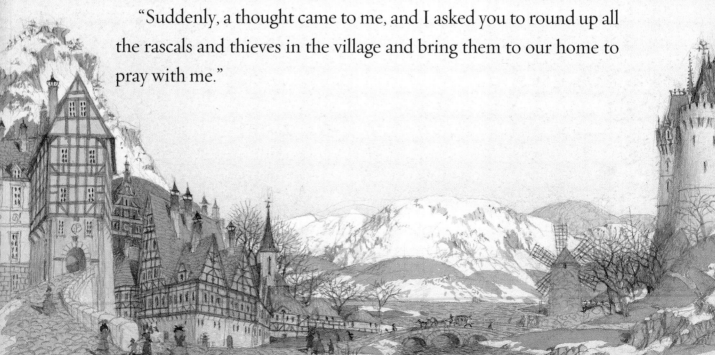

"And then what happened?" asked Pavel, who was still confused. "How did you unlock the gates?"

The old man smiled his biggest smile and said, "When I prayed the second time, I had a band of thieves to assist me. A good thief knows how to break in and enter, my dear Pavel. But this time they did it with prayers, and their prayers provided the key to opening the gates.

"You see, the thieves represent the things in us that are bad or wrong or selfish – the parts we need to change to be happy. When we want to make miracles happen, we have to recognize and acknowledge our bad traits. And when we turn away from our naughty behaviour and embrace good deeds, as the thieves did with their prayers, we are turning the key and unlocking the gates of Heaven. And then we can receive blessings and good fortune."

"Oh, I see," said Pavel, finally understanding.

The wise old man stood up, looked down at his grandson's bare feet, and said, "Now, go and try on your new shoes. I am going to get some rest."

Suddenly, there was a loud knock at the door. Pavel jumped to open it but did not see anyone there.

"Yoo-hoo, down here!" said someone with a very gruff voice.

Pavel looked down, and there was Boris the Barefoot Midget with a guilty look on his face.

"I think these belong to you," said Boris. And from behind his back he produced a pair of worn sandals. "I accidentally took them from your house last night. They must have fallen into my pocket, and I aahhhhh . . . uuuumm . . . errrrrrrr . . . do not really need them so . . . aaaaahhhhhhh . . . uummmmmm . . . errrr . . . please accept my apology."

"I accept, but you can keep them," replied Pavel, looking down at his new green shoes. "I won't be needing them any more."

Boris felt shy. He stepped into the sandals, said "Thank you" for the first time in his life, and scurried down the road.

Pavel laughed as he watched him go.

PUFFIN BOOKS

Published by the Penguin Group: London, New York, Australia,
Canada, India, New Zealand and South Africa
Penguin Books Ltd, Registered Offices: 80 Strand, London WC2R 0RL, England

www.penguin.com

First published in Great Britain in Puffin Books 2004
3 5 7 9 10 8 6 4 2
Designed by Toshiya Masuda and produced by Callaway Editions, New York
www.callaway.com
The moral right of the author and illustrator has been asserted
Made and printed in Italy
ISBN 0–141–38049–7

Visit Madonna at www.madonna.com

All of Madonna's proceeds from this book will be donated to the Spirituality for Kids Foundation.

MADONNA RITCHIE was born in Bay City, Michigan, and has seven brothers and sisters. She has sold 200 million
albums worldwide and has had more than 25 Top Ten singles. She is the recipient of three Grammys, as well as a
Golden Globe award for her performance in *Evita*. She lives with her husband, movie director Guy Ritchie, and her
two children, Lola and Rocco, in London and Los Angeles. Her previous children's books, *The English Roses*
and *Mr Peabody's Apples* – released in 40 languages in more than 100 countries – are international bestsellers.

GENNADY SPIRIN was born on Christmas Day in a small city near Moscow. He has illustrated 33 children's books.
He has received four gold medals from the Society of Illustrators, the Golden Apple and the Grand Prix from the
Bratislava and Barcelona International Biennials, respectively, and the first prize at the Bologna International Book Fair.
Mr Spirin lives in New Jersey with his wife and three sons.

A NOTE ON THE TYPE:

This book is set in Requiem, a font derived from a set of inscriptional capitals appearing in
Ludovico Vicentino degli Arrighi's 1523 writing manual, *Il Modo de Temperare le Penne*. A master scribe,
Arrighi is remembered as an exemplar of the chancery italic, a style revived in Requiem's italic.